Everyone had high hopes for Mike.

Miss Young wanted him to become a scientist.

The GREAT ROCK'N'ROLL MYSTERY

Written by Roy Wandelmaier

Illustrated by Raymond Burns

Troll Associates

Library of Congress Cataloging in Publication Data

Wandelmaier, Roy.
  The great rock 'n' roll mystery.

   Summary: A boy yearns to play the saxophone. He and his
sister, and his dog become involved with bank robbers
and a famous saxophonist.
   1. Children's stories, American. [1. Mystery and
detective stories] I. Burns, Raymond, 1924-   ill.
II. Title.
PZ7.W179Gr   1985   [E]   84-8753
ISBN 0-8167-0416-3 (lib. bdg.)
ISBN 0-8167-0417-1 (pbk.)

The GREAT ROCK'N'ROLL MYSTERY

His father wanted him to become a
banker. His mother wanted her son to
become a doctor.

Mike, however, just wanted to play the saxophone. He wanted to become as great a player as his hero, Memphis Malone.

"We can't afford a saxophone," said Mike's father at breakfast, "because that Dudley of yours is driving us to the poor farm!"

"G-r-r-r," growled Dudley from the back yard.

Mike's father was always trying to come up with a good reason to give away their dog. But Mike and his sister Annie always defended him.

"Dudley's part of the family, Dad," said Annie.

"Dudley is the enemy!" said Dad.
"He eats too much. He chases the mailman.
He gobbles up your mother's flowers.

"But yesterday was the last straw.
That animal of yours chewed up the seat
of my favorite chair. If he doesn't start
to behave, I'm sending him away."

"Dad!" cried Mike and Annie.

Maybe Dudley wasn't the best, but he was theirs.

That morning, Mike, Annie, and Dudley walked down to the music store on the corner. On the way, four older boys passed by in a car. One rolled down his window and said, "Where did you ever get such an ugly dog?"

"G-r-r-r," growled Dudley.

Annie and Mike ignored the boys and kept walking.

It's going to be a long summer, thought Mike.

When they got to the music store, Mike stopped to look at the shiny new saxophone. But that day there was also something new in the window—a poster. It said that Memphis Malone was giving a concert that night at Foley Square. Mike and Annie were thrilled.

Then something else happened. Across the street, two masked men ran out of the bank and into an alley. Alarms rang. People came out onto the street.

"Stop them," cried Mrs. Horn, the bank's owner. "We've been robbed!"

When the police arrived, Chief Owens said, "Don't worry, Mrs. Horn. The town is sealed off. We'll find them."

Mrs. Horn offered a big reward.

"This is our chance," whispered Mike. "We can find those robbers, if we just think like detectives."

First they searched the bakery. Then they carefully watched people enter the super-market. They each had a sundae at Danny's 1,001 Dairy Delights, but they didn't spot any bank robbers.

Later they checked the laundromat and
Billy's Gas Station, but they had no luck.
"It's no use," said Mike.

"Cheer up," said Annie. "At least we can go see Memphis Malone tonight."

Dudley wagged his tail.

"Of course we're taking you, partner," she said.

That night, Mike and Annie were too excited to finish their dinner. When their mother wasn't looking, and their father went into the kitchen to get his tea, they slipped their plates to Dudley under the table.

After dinner, they got their bikes from
the garage. Dudley ran alongside Mike.
But they did not tell their parents where
they were going.

When they got to Foley Square, the
guards would not let Dudley in.

"No dogs allowed," they said. Dudley
tried to wag his tail, but anyone could see his
feelings were hurt.

Luckily it was an outdoor concert. "Don't worry, Dudley," said Mike. They walked behind the bleachers and sat down. They couldn't *see* Memphis Malone, but they heard him fine.

Memphis and his band played well that
night. By the end of the concert, everyone
was clapping and the stars were twinkling.

Mike, Annie, and Dudley walked to the backstage entrance. Time passed slowly, and most of the other fans went home.

"We'd better go home too, Mike," said Annie. "Mom and Dad will wonder where we are."

Just then the band appeared. But something looked wrong to Mike. Who were those other men?

"Memphis!" cried Annie.

"Can we have your autograph?" asked Mike.

"He doesn't have time," said one of the strangers.

"Just one?" asked Memphis Malone.

"All right, but hurry!"

"Please write 'for Dudley'—he's our dog," said Mike.

Malone smiled. He scribbled something on a note pad and gave it to Mike. Then Memphis Malone, his band, and the strange men got into a van and drove away.

"Oh, man," said Annie.
"Oh, wow," said Mike.
"Ar-rooo!" said Dudley.

Mike looked at the autograph, but it
didn't say what any of them expected.
"*Help,*" it said. "*Robbers—airport.*"

Then Mike knew what was wrong.
"Those men were the bank robbers, Annie!
They're forcing Memphis to drive them out of
town. The police will never look in his van!"
"Let's head them off," said Annie.

They hopped onto their bikes and flew down the hill. Across the field they rode, then behind the bank and onto Third Street. There, pulling up to a red light, was Memphis Malone's van.

Mike and Annie were scared, but they
rode their bikes up to the van anyway.

"Hi," said Annie to the man at the wheel.
She tried to smile.

"Beat it," said the man.

"What an ugly dog," said his friend.
"G-r-r-r," growled Dudley.

The light turned to green. Then the whole street seemed to explode.

Dudley leaped after the van. RRRIPPPP!

A tire blew. A woman screamed for help.
Lights flashed. The van lurched, then roared
down the street.

Then things really went crazy. Fire
alarms rang. A police car flew by and pulled
over the limping van.

The police arrested the robbers.

Mike, Annie, and Dudley ran over.
Memphis Malone and the band were slowly
getting out of the van.

"Man, that was wild!" said Memphis.
"Hey," he said to the police officers,
"these are the kids that saved us. Thanks,
you guys."

The next day, Mike, Annie, and Dudley were heroes. The mayor gave a speech in their honor. Mrs. Horn gave them their reward.

"Those are our children," beamed Mike and Annie's mom.

"And don't they have a terrific dog?" said Chief Owens.

"Well, sometimes," Dad admitted. He patted Dudley on the head.

Miss Young advised Annie and Mike to donate their money to science.

Their father wanted them to invest it in the stock market.

But Annie and Mike first bought their father a new chair, and their mother a beautiful new vase. Annie spent the rest of her reward to buy a guitar. Mike spent the rest of his on the shiny new saxophone.

And guess who gave them their first
lesson?

It was going to be a great summer.